SOCCER
LAWS
ILLUSTRATED

SOCCER LAWS ILLUSTRATED

Officially approved and recommended by
THE REFEREES' COMMITTEE OF F.I.F.A.

Stanley Lover

With
THE LAWS OF THE GAME
and
DECISIONS OF THE INTERNATIONAL
FOOTBALL ASSOCIATION BOARD

Revised 1984 and 1988

Reproduction authorised by
FEDERATION INTERNATIONALE DE FOOTBALL ASSOCIATION
F.I.F.A.

PELHAM BOOKS

PELHAM BOOKS

Published by the Penguin Group
27 Wrights Lane, London w8 5tz, England
Viking Penguin Inc., 40 West 23rd Street, New York, New York 10010, USA
Penguin Books Australia Ltd, Ringwood, Victoria, Australia
Penguin Books Canada Ltd, 2801 John Street, Markham, Ontario, Canada l3r 1b4
Penguin Books (NZ) Ltd, 182–190 Wairau Road, Auckland 10, New Zealand

Penguin Books Ltd, Registered Offices: Harmondsworth, Middlesex, England

First published by Pelham Books 1971
Reprinted 1971, 1976, 1977
Revised paperback edition 1984
Reprinted 1985
Second Revised edition 1988

British Library Cataloguing in Publication Data

Lover, Stanley
Soccer laws illustrated. – Rev. ed.
1. Soccer laws – Rules
I. Title
769.334′02′022

ISBN 0 7207 1852 X

Printed and bound in Great Britain by
Hollen Street Press Ltd, Slough, Berkshire

CONTENTS

FOREWORD
by

Sir Stanley Rous C.B.E.

I am pleased to write a foreword to this book because, it will help the many thousands of football followers throughout the world to understand the Laws of the Game. Referees know them, but many players do not know what they may or may not do on the field of play.

Visual aids are the easiest way of teaching; television, films, diagrams and charts are available to help to educate the public and this book will certainly do so with its "problem" diagrams.

There is a minimum of explanation to emphasize the essential point of each law. The author has taken care to base the text on the official wording of the Laws and Decisions of The International Board. The whole of the game is covered in a logical arrangement and will appeal, I hope, to players at all levels, referees, coaches, club officials and to spectators.

The author of this work, Mr. Stanley Lover, knows the needs of followers of the game, having been a player, a referee, a lecturer and an administrator. This contribution to the text books of Association Football should have a wide circulation.

STANLEY ROUS,
Honorary President,
F.I.F.A.
(died 1986)

7

PREFACE
by

Ken Aston

Football as we know it today has been played for well over 100 years. The International Board (who make the laws) have always been careful not to confuse footballers and spectators by continually making changes to the 17 Laws. This is why it is possible to play matches between teams from different continents of the world without any real difficulties about the way the game should be played.

Most footballers and spectators have a general grasp of the basic laws, but the more they are understood the more pleasure people will get from the game. Players who do not understand the laws may feel unfairly treated by the referee.

A referee must have a complete knowledge of all the laws and the many official decisions relating to them, as well as a true understanding of the spirit of the game. It cannot be expected that players and spectators should have such an expert knowledge and the text of this book is not intended to deal with the laws in such detail. The official Laws are included however, for readers who wish to broaden their knowledge.

Those who have studied the Laws are often surprised to see an apparent offence ignored by the referee. Much is left to the 'opinion' of the referee especially when he has to decide between what is intentional and what is accidental; his nearness to the incident helps him to form a better judgment. He may also see an offence but think it of more advantage to let play continue than to stop play and give the offended team a free-kick.

The referee is human and therefore makes mistakes – but he makes fewer than is generally supposed. This you will see for yourself as you follow the book through. At the end, you will find yourself a better player and a more knowledgeable spectator.

KEN ASTON,
Past Chairman F.I.F.A. Referees'
Committee and member of
the International Board

The Spirit Of The Game

Football is more than a simple game. It is an emotional experience.

The mechanics of play amount to the movement of a ball, about the size of a man's head, between two targets set some distance apart. But, during the course of just one game, the whole range of human emotions from the depths of despair to utter joy can be touched in the hearts of those who play or watch.

Somewhere in these emotions lies the key to the Spirit of the Game, a term often mentioned but seldom defined. Merely to present in these pages a series of illustrations of the written rules, or laws, without considering the spirit in which they are intended to be applied would be a grave omission.

Few major alterations to the original Laws have been found necessary, which emphasises the wisdom of the founders of the modern game. A close look at the reasoning behind the Laws provides three important clues to the interpretation of the Spirit of the Game, which early and subsequent legislators have followed.

Firstly, all players must have an equal opportunity to demonstrate individual skills without undue interference from opponents. Physical size is not an essential requirement for success. A player of small stature can contribute as much by quick reactions and great manoeuvrability as one whose assets include height and strength. Many players of small physique have achieved world wide fame by demonstrating their exciting skills.

Secondly, much stress is laid on the safety of players in normal match play. In specifying the size of the playing area, components used and equipment of players care is taken to eliminate anything which may prove dangerous.

Thirdly, the Laws are specific on punishments for infringements and misconduct. It is clearly implied that the game is intended to be played within a code of conduct based on accepted principles of mutual respect between people from all walks of life. Only by observing these principles can the game be played with maximum enjoyment.

Summarising then, the main features of the Spirit of the Game are simply EQUALITY, SAFETY AND ENJOYMENT.

From time to time the International Football Association Board receive suggestions for improving the Game and alterations to the Laws. Recently the Board made the following statement which needs no further comment:—

> 'It is the belief of the Board that the Spirit in which the Game is played is of paramount importance and that changes in the Laws to improve the Game as a spectacle are of little value if "fair play" is not universally observed.'

STANLEY F. LOVER

Section 1

COMPONENTS

Components

In sports where competitors are required to demonstrate their skills it is important that any equipment used is as standard as can be devised. Any unequal factor will detract from the interest and enjoyment of the contest.

Such equipment must also be designed to minimise elements of danger to the competitors and yet encourage maximum effort.

In Football much thought has been devoted to the basic components common to all organised matches no matter where they may be played.

The first four Laws of the Game detail these components.

Football is played on a rectangular field to encourage the flow of play between the main targets i.e. the goals.

The size of the field may be varied between given limits according to the space available. However, the named areas within the boundaries are of fixed dimensions.

The field is divided into two equal halves.

Goal nets are advisable but not compulsory.

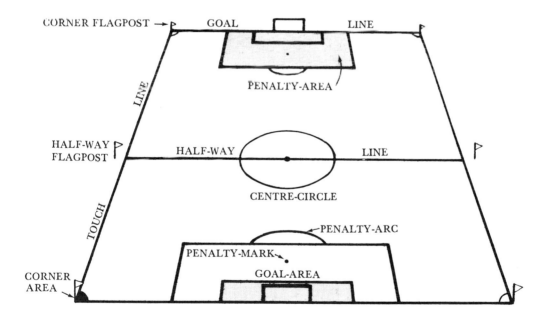

THE FIELD OF PLAY, SHOWING THE PENALTY, GOAL AND CORNER AREAS SHADED.

The size of the goal is related to the physical capability of the goalkeeper to defend the goal and to demand skill from attacking players to score.

The goalposts are usually white in colour so they can easily be seen.

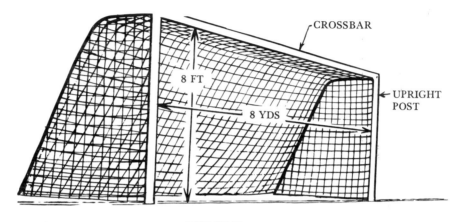

CROSSBAR

8 FT

8 YDS

UPRIGHT POST

THE GOAL.

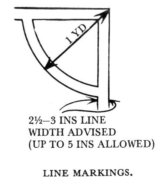

1 YD

2½–3 INS LINE WIDTH ADVISED (UP TO 5 INS ALLOWED)

LINE MARKINGS.

5 FT MIN.

CORNER FLAGPOST

(COMPULSORY)

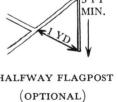

5 FT MIN.

1 YD

HALFWAY FLAGPOST

(OPTIONAL)

(For metric measurements see Page 103)

If, during a game, a crossbar is broken may it be replaced by a rope?

Only by mutual consent of the teams in a match not played under competitive rules. Otherwise a rope is not considered a satisfactory substitute. (Decision No. 8).

Flagposts shorter than 5 feet (1.50 m.) are dangerous.

A spherical ball is chosen for the playing of Association Football because it truly reflects the skill of the player in kicking, heading or moving it in any manner permitted by the Laws.

Its size, weight, pressure, materials used in construction are rigidly specified for equality and safety.

27–28
INCHES

THE BALL.

May the winning team keep the ball at the end of the match?

May the ball be changed during a game?

'The ball shall not be changed during the game unless authorized by the Referee'. (Law 2).

'The ball is considered to be the property of the Association or Club on whose ground the match is played, and at the close of play it must be returned to the Referee'. (Decision No. 1).

In every match there are two teams, each having not more than eleven players. Where the competition rules permit up to two substitutes may be used.

One member of each team shall be a goalkeeper with the special privilege of handling the ball within his team's penalty area.

A team starts a match with only ten players. The eleventh player arrives at the commencement of the second half. May he join his team ?

Yes, provided that the Referee is advised. If the game is in progress the player must wait for a signal from the Referee.

A goalkeeper is injured and wishes to change places with another player. Is this permitted?

Yes, at any time provided that the referee is advised when the change is to be made.

May a player, who has had to leave the field for treatment of an injury, return to his team?

Yes, after receiving a signal from the referee.

Components

What is the correct procedure for a substitute to join the game?

The Referee must be informed if a player is to be substituted. A substitute may only be permitted to enter the field of play during a stoppage in the game and after he has received a signal from the Referee authorising him to do so. The substitute must enter the field of play at the halfway line after the player he is replacing has left.

If a player is dismissed from the game because of misconduct, may his place be taken by a substitute (No. 12)?

'A player who has been ordered off **before** play begins may only be replaced by one of the named substitutes'.

'A player who has been ordered off **after** play has started may not be replaced'. (Decision No. 3).

The main points of this law are:—

(a) 'A player shall not wear anything which is dangerous to another player'.

(b) 'A goalkeeper shall wear colours which distinguish him from the other players and from the Referee'.

½ IN DIAMETER
MINIMUM

(³/₈ IN WHEN STUDS
ARE MOULDED INTO
THE SOLE — MINIMUM
NUMBER 10 STUDS)

¾ IN MAXIMUM

NAILS MUST BE DRIVEN
FLUSH WITH SURFACE

Boots are normally worn to protect the feet. They may also have bars or studs added to obtain a secure foothold. These must conform to rigid standards to reduce the element of danger to other players.

Can any action be taken if a player advises the Referee that an injury has been caused by the studs on an opponent's boot?

The Referee has power to examine players' boots and to prevent any player, whose boots are considered dangerous, from taking further part in the game until they have been corrected or replaced. (See Decision No. 3).

The Referee may require a player to remove a ring or any other article which could cause injury.

May a person who wears spectacles play football?

The Laws do not prohibit spectacles, but the wearer must understand that he plays at his own risk.

A player decides to discard his boots and play without any footwear. Is this permitted?

'The Law does not insist that boots or shoes must be worn. However, in competition matches, Referees should not allow one or a few players to play without footwear when all the other players are so equipped'. (Decision No. 2).

When a player has had to leave the field to correct some item of equipment, how may he rejoin the game?

The player must wait for a stoppage in the game before reporting to the Referee who will then examine the players equipment and satisfy himself that it is in order. (See Decision No. 5).

What would happen if a player, who has left the field with the Referee's permission to correct dangerous equipment, rejoins the game without waiting for play to be stopped?

The Referee is required to caution the player. (See Decision No. 6). An indirect free-kick is awarded to the opposing team.

Section 2

LAWS OF PLAY

Laws of Play

This Section outlines the nine Laws which state the procedure to be followed in the timing of the game, how to commence play, when it should be stopped, how it is to be restarted, and method of scoring, etc.

The time allowed for playing the game provides ample opportunity for demonstrating skills and for enjoyment without damaging the health of the players.

The normal period of play is 90 minutes made up of two equal periods of 45 minutes. These periods may be slightly reduced for young players. Where competition rules allow, extra time may be played in the event of there being no result at the end of the normal period.

When a game is delayed to allow an injured player to receive treatment, or to be removed from the field, the Referee will add time to compensate for the amount lost.

As the Referee is about to signal the end of play a defender handles the ball in his own penalty-area. What action must the Referee take?

A penalty kick must be awarded.

The Referee has authority to extend playing time to allow a penalty kick to be taken at the end of a normal period. (Law 7.b).

If, at the end of the first period of play the visiting team's captain asks the Referee to commence the second period without an interval, so that his team can start their return journey as early as possible, would this be in order?

'Players have a right to an interval at half-time'. (Decision No. 2). The Referee could not agree to the request unless all players gave their consent.

Each team defends one half of the field. The toss of a coin decides which team chooses the half it wishes to defend, and which team is to have first possession of the ball.

At the end of the half-time interval the teams exchange ends. The kick-off to commence the second period goes to the team which did not have it at the beginning of the game.

The kick-off is taken to commence play, after a goal is scored and after half-time. To re-start the game after a temporary stoppage through any cause, not mentioned elsewhere in the Laws, the Referee will drop the ball.

As a spectator is it possible to know which team won the toss by the way the teams are arranged at the start of the game?

No, because the captain winning the toss may decide to have first possession of the ball, i.e. the kick-off. The losing captain would then decide which end of the field to defend.

Where should players stand at the kick-off?

Every player shall be in his own half of the field and every player of the team opposing that of the kicker shall remain not less than 10 yards from the ball until it has travelled the distance of its circumference. (Law 8.a).

May a player kick the ball before it touches the ground when it is being dropped by the Referee?

No. The ball is not in play until it touches the ground. In this case the Referee would drop the ball again. (Law 8.d).

The boundary lines i.e. goal-lines and touch-lines, contain the game within a reasonable area to encourage the flow of play between the goal targets.

The ball is out of play, and the game brought to a halt, when the whole of the ball has crossed over a boundary line, either on the ground or in the air.

The lines belong to the areas of which they are the boundaries.

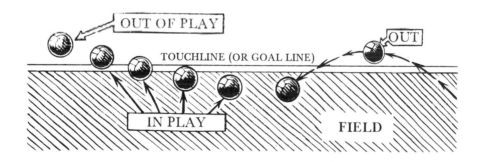

Should play be stopped if the ball strikes the Referee?

No. Law 9 states that the ball is in play 'If it rebounds off either the Referee or Linesman when they are in the field of play'.

In the case shown here a goal would be awarded.

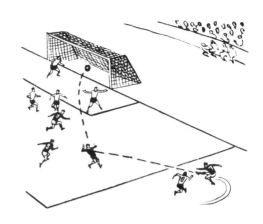

If the ball goes over the goal line, but is caught by the goalkeeper who is standing in the field of play, must the game be stopped?

Yes, if the ball has passed completely over the goal line. The position of the goalkeeper does not alter this fact.

'The team scoring the greater number of goals during a game shall be the winner; if no goals, or an equal number of goals are scored, the game shall be termed a "draw" '.

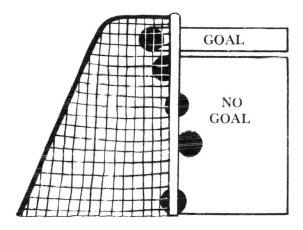

To score a goal, the whole of the ball must pass over the goal-line, between the posts and under the crossbar.

If the ball is about to enter the goal but is deflected by a dog (or spectator) can the Referee award a goal?

No. The Referee must restart the game by dropping the ball at the place where the interference occurred. (See Decision No. 2).

Would a goal be scored if a goalkeeper, standing in his own penalty-area, throws the ball with the aid of a strong wind, into his opponents goal without any other player touching the ball?

Yes. This is the only way in which an attacking player can score by the use of the hands.

34

Free-kicks may be awarded by the Referee during the course of play, to penalise teams infringing the Laws. 'Free' means free from interference by the offending team whose players must promptly move away to the proper distance from the ball.

There are two types of free-kick:

(a)   DIRECT—a goal can be scored direct, but only against the offending team.

(b)   INDIRECT—after being kicked the ball must be touched or played by another player, of either team, before a goal can be scored.

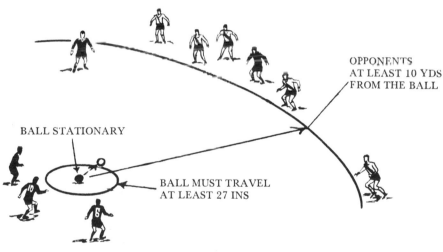

OPPONENTS
AT LEAST 10 YDS
FROM THE BALL

BALL STATIONARY

BALL MUST TRAVEL
AT LEAST 27 INS

TEAM-MATES MAY STAND
NEARER THAN 10 YDS

POSITION OF PLAYERS AT A FREE-KICK.

If a defending player takes a Direct free-kick from outside his penalty-area, and kicks the ball past his own goalkeeper into the goal, what would be the correct decision?

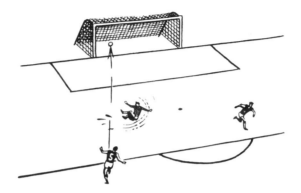

The Referee would award a corner-kick to the attacking team, because a goal can only be scored against the offending team from a direct free-kick.

How do players and spectators know if the free-kick is direct or indirect?

When the Referee awards an indirect free-kick he signals it by raising his arm. This signal precedes the blowing of the whistle for the free-kick to be taken; no such signal is given in the case of a direct free-kick. (See Decision No. 1).

May the defending players stand less than 10 yards from the ball at any time?

Only when an indirect free-kick is to be taken from a position less than 10 yards from the goal. Defenders may stand on the goal line between the posts.

Is it in order for defending players to move nearer than 10 yards when the signal is given?

Not until the ball has been kicked into play, i.e. after it has travelled the distance of its circumference — 27 to 28 ins.

If the defending team is awarded a free-kick inside their own penalty area, is it in order for the ball to be played to the goalkeeper?

No. The ball is not in play until it has passed outside the penalty area. The kick would be retaken.

From an indirect free-kick the ball strikes the crossbar, hits the goalkeeper and bounces over the goal-line. Would this be a goal?

Yes, because the ball was last played by a player other than the kicker before it entered the goal.

A penalty-kick is an important award to punish any of the nine offences specified in Law 12, if intentionally committed by a player of the defending team within his own penalty-area.

Law 14 describes the requirements for the taking of a penalty-kick. These include restrictions on the conduct of the kicker, goalkeeper, defenders and attackers.

When time is extended to allow a penalty-kick to be taken the extension shall last until the kick has been completed as described in Decisions No. 6 and 7.

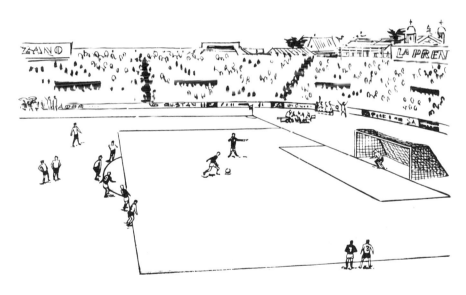

POSITIONS OF PLAYERS AT A PENALTY-KICK

'. . . all players with the exception of the player taking the kick, and the opposing goalkeeper, shall be within the field of play but outside the penalty-area, and at least 10 yards from the penalty-mark.'

The Referee has given the signal for the penalty to be taken but, before the ball is kicked, a defender moves into the penalty-area. What is the correct procedure?

The Referee will not delay the kick. If a goal is scored, it will be allowed. If a goal is not scored the kick must be retaken. Encroaching is considered to be misconduct. The defender would be cautioned. (Decision No. 3c).

What would happen if a player of each team encroaches into the penalty-area or within 10 yards of the penalty-mark before the ball is in play?

The penalty-kick must be retaken and the players concerned will be cautioned. (Decision No. 5b).

40

If the goalkeeper moves before the penalty-kick is taken will the Referee stop the kick?

No. He will await the result of the kick. If a goal is scored it will be allowed. If not the kick must be retaken. (See Decision No. 3b).

Would a goal be allowed if the ball strikes the crossbar or goalpost and returns to the kicker who then kicks it into goal?

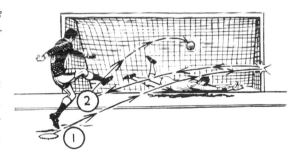

A goal would not be allowed because the kicker must not play the ball a second time until it has been touched by another player. The Referee would award an indirect free-kick against the kicker.

The Referee has extended time to allow a penalty-kick to be taken. If the ball rebounds from the goalkeeper to the kicker, who scores, will the goal be allowed?

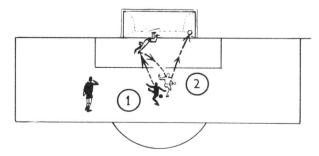

No. The game ends the moment the goalkeeper prevents the ball from entering the goal.

When the ball crosses a touch-line the game is restarted by a throw-in awarded to the team opposite to that of the player who last touched the ball.

It is the only occasion when players, other than the goalkeepers, may handle the ball, intentionally, without being penalised.

A goal shall not be scored direct from a throw-in.

CORRECT THROW-IN.
FACING FIELD OF PLAY.
BOTH FEET ON GROUND,
ON OR BEHIND LINE.

INCORRECT. ONLY
ONE FOOT ON GROUND.

INCORRECT. ONLY
ONE HAND
THROWING BALL.

CORRECT. BOTH
HANDS THROWING
BALL.

Is it in order to take a quick throw-in from behind the touch-line opposite to the point where it left play?

BALL LEAVES
PLAY HERE

The ball must be thrown-in from the point where it crossed the touch-line, not as shown.

Is this throw-in correct?..

Yes, provided that the ball is thrown from behind and over the head, and that the action of throwing is continuous from the start of the throw to the point of release.

43

When one of the attacking team plays the ball over the goal-line, excluding the portion between the goalposts, the defending team is awarded a goal-kick.

The ball is not in play until it has been kicked direct out of the penalty-area.

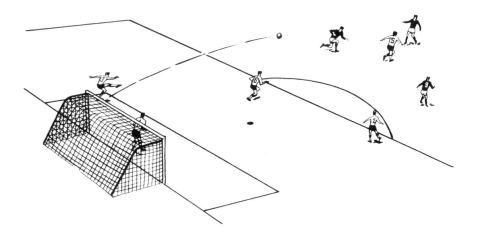

CORRECT GOAL-KICK.

Attackers outside penalty-area; ball leaving penalty-area having been kicked from the half of the goal-area nearest to where the ball crossed the goal-line.

If the ball should be played again before it leaves the penalty-area, the goal-kick must be retaken.

If the ball is kicked over the goal-line before it has cleared the penalty-area, should the Referee award a corner-kick?

Because the ball was not in play when it crossed the goal-line, the goal-kick would be retaken.

When one of the defending team plays the ball over the goal line, excluding the portion between the goalposts, the attacking team is awarded a corner-kick.

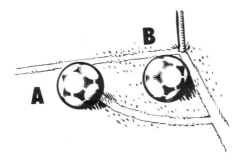

BALL POSITION IN CORNER-AREA.

A is not correctly placed because it is not wholly within the quarter circle.

B is correct.

Would it be in order for the kicker to move the corner-flag post?

The corner-area provides ample room for a player to take a corner-kick. The flag-post must not be moved.

Which positions may attackers and defenders take in relation to the ball at a corner-kick.

Attackers may be as near to the ball as they wish, but defenders must be at least 10 yards away.

If the ball is kicked against a goal post and returns to the kicker, may he then play it again?

The kicker may not play the ball a second time until it has been touched by another player. An indirect free-kick would be awarded where the ball was played for the second time by the kicker.

If the ball goes directly into goal from a corner-kick would a goal be allowed?

Yes.

If the ball swerves over the goal-line but back into play, should the game continue?

The moment the whole of the ball has crossed the goal-line it is out of play. The game would be stopped and a goal-kick awarded to the defending team.

Section 3

OFF-SIDE
AND
FOUL PLAY

Off-side and Foul Play

Of the seventeen Laws two which deserve special study are Laws 11 and 12.

Law 11 deals with Off-side and is the only law concerned with tactical play.

Law 12, entitled Fouls and Misconduct, provides safeguards for players in discouraging unnecessary physical force and rough play. It is also intended to preserve the good name of football by defining acts of misconduct against the Spirit of the Game.

This law is designed to discourage uninteresting play by attacking players. The game could be played without Law 11 but it could lead to players standing close to goal waiting for the ball for short range attempts at scoring. Such play would require little skill or ability.

It is not a difficult law to understand if two basic points are clearly established. They are:—

(a) A matter of FACT based on the actual position of the player **at the moment the ball is played** by one of his own side and,

(b) A matter of OPINION judged by his influence on the play and his motive for being in that position.

Off-side.
Examples.

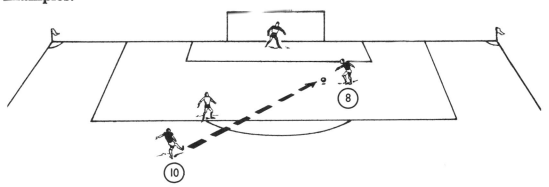

When No. 10 passes the ball forward No. 8 is off-side because he is in front of the ball and does not have two opponents nearer the goal-line.

The ball is passed to No. 9 who is standing in line with defender No. 2. No. 9 is off-side because he is in front of the ball and had only one opponent (the goalkeeper) nearer the goal-line when the ball was played.

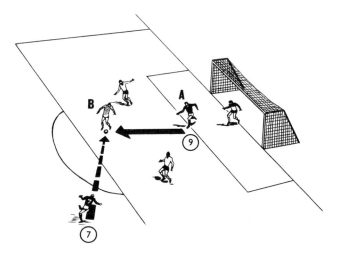

When No. 7 passes the ball No. 9 is standing in position A. He runs back to receive the ball at position B but is off-side for the same reasons as in the previous example.

A player cannot put himself on-side by running back.

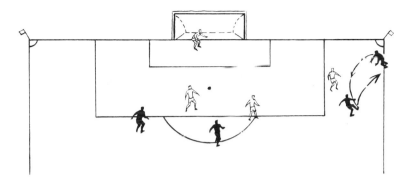

The ball is thrown-in and immediately played back to the thrower, who is now off-side, being in front of the ball and not having two or more opponents nearer the goal-line.

No. 8 shoots for goal. The ball rebounds from the crossbar to No. 11. Although No. 11 was behind the ball when it hit the crossbar he was off-side the moment No. 8 played the ball, not having two opponents nearer the goal-line. It is the equivalent of a direct pass.

53

The ball is kicked into goal but No. 7, in an off-side position, would be judged to be interfering with play by obstructing or distracting the goalkeeper. The goal would not be allowed.

Not Off-side.

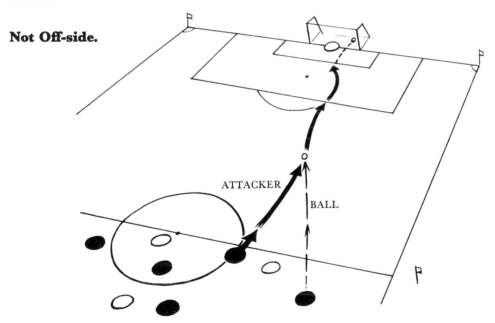

A player cannot be off-side within his own half of the field of play.

In this case the attacker has run forward into the opponents half **after** the ball was played.

Off-side and Foul Play

Off-side.

No. 8 kicks the ball towards the goal but it is deflected by a defender to No. 9 who scores. The goal is not allowed because No. 9 was in an off-side position at the moment the ball was kicked by No. 8. The deflection by the defender in this case does not affect the basic principles of off-side.

Not Off-side.
Examples.

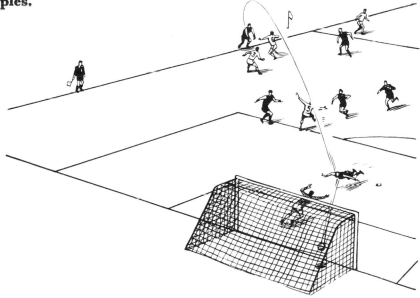

A player cannot be off-side if he receives the ball from a throw-in. The goal would be allowed.

No. 9 is not off-side because he was not in front of the ball when it was last played by a team-mate.

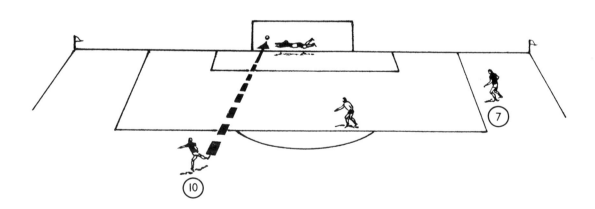

No. 10 shoots the ball into goal, but No. 7 is standing in an off-side position. However, because he is well away from play opponent No. 7 would not be penalised for off-side. The goal would be allowed.

Off-side and Foul Play

A player cannot be off-side
if he receives the ball direct
from a corner-kick

No. 7 has run on to the ball from a forward pass. No. 7 was not in front of the ball when last played by his team-mate; he is therefore not off-side.

Summarising the Off-side Law. In every possible situation only two questions need answering:—

(i)   Is the player in an off-side position when the ball is played by one of his own side? (This is a matter of FACT).

(ii) Is he interfering with play (or opponent) or trying to gain an advantage? (This is a matter of OPINION).

If the answer is 'Yes' then,

The underlying 'Spirit of the Game', described earlier, can be clearly seen throughout the whole of this Law. Not only does it define physical acts against opponents which are undesirable, but it also establishes the code of conduct expected from players and officials to safeguard the welfare of the game.

Law 12 comprises three parts:—

> (i)   Major Offences
> (ii)   Other Offences
> (iii) Misconduct

(i) **Major Offences:**

There are nine major offences which, if committed **intentionally,** are penalised by the award of a Direct Free-Kick to the opposing team.

Eight of the nine are concerned with physical acts against opponents.

Should a player of the defending team intentionally commit any one of the nine offences within the penalty-area, when the ball is in play, a penalty-kick will be awarded to the opposing team.

Examples of Major Offences

KICKING AN OPPONENT.

TRIPPING—USING THE LEGS.

TRIPPING—BY STOOPING IN FRONT OF (OR BEHIND) AN OPPONENT.

JUMPING AT AN OPPONENT.
(The offending player clearly has no intention of playing the ball.)

CHARGING IN A VIOLENT OR DANGEROUS MANNER.

A CHARGE IN THE BACK CAN
CAUSE SERIOUS INJURY.

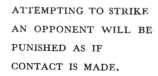

ATTEMPTING TO STRIKE
AN OPPONENT WILL BE
PUNISHED AS IF
CONTACT IS MADE.

A GOALKEEPER WHO INTENTIONALLY THROWS THE BALL AT AN OPPONENT IS GUILTY
OF STRIKING.

HOLDING WITH THE HAND OR ARM.

PULLING AN OPPONENT'S SHIRT IS CONSIDERED TO BE HOLDING.

PUSHING AN OPPONENT.

HANDLING THE BALL WITH ANY PART OF THE HAND OR ARM. (THIS DOES NOT APPLY TO THE GOALKEEPER IN HIS OWN PENALTY AREA.)

AN EXAMPLE OF A FOUL TACKLE FROM BEHIND WHICH MAY BE INTERPRETED AS KICKING OR TRIPPING.

AN EXAMPLE OF A 'FOOT OVER' TACKLE, WHICH IS DANGEROUS AND MAY BE INTERPRETED AS KICKING.

63

Fair charge.

An example of a **fair charge,** shoulder to shoulder, ball within playing distance, arms and elbows tucked in. It is fair to attempt to put an opponent off-balance, with a fair charge, when trying to obtain possession of the ball.

Unintentional handling.

An example of unintentional handling where the ball is kicked onto the hand. This is not an offence.

(ii) **Other Offences:**

There are six main offences, under this heading, for which an Indirect free-kick is awarded to the opposing team. These are:—

(a) dangerous play,

(b) charging fairly but at the wrong moment,

(c) obstruction,

(d) charging the goalkeeper (with three exceptions),

(e) excessive possession of the ball by the goalkeeper,

(f) timewasting tactics by the goal-keeper,

Examples of Other Offences

(a) **Dangerous play**

Attempting to kick the ball held by the goalkeeper (dangerous play).

An overhead 'bicycle' kick or a 'scissor' kick, shown here, may be interpreted as dangerous play if attempted near other players.

(b) **Charging at wrong moment.**

Attempting to kick a ball near the head of an opponent is dangerous.

Fair charge but the ball is not within playing distance.

(c) **Obstruction.**

An example of 'screening' the ball from an opponent which is **not obstruction** because the ball is being played.

Obstruction is penalised when a player blocks the opponents path to the ball when it is not within playing distance.

Obstruction by running between an opponent and the ball.

(d) **Charging goalkeeper**

Charging the goalkeeper in his goal-area when he is not holding the ball or obstructing an opponent is an offence.

(e) **Possession by goalkeeper**

The goalkeeper is allowed no more than four steps while holding, bouncing or throwing the ball in the air before releasing it. After releasing the ball the goalkeeper is not allowed to touch it again with his hands until it has been played by another player. He may, however, play the ball with his feet.

68

(iii) **Misconduct:**

Any player who intentionally disregards the principles of the Laws of the Game by acts of discourtesy to officials, persistently breaking the Laws, or whose conduct offends the accepted code of proper behaviour will receive an official caution.

For acts of violent conduct, foul or abusive language or repeated misconduct after being cautioned, players will be immediately dismissed from the game.

Misconduct of any kind requiring the above action must be reported to the appropriate authority. Further disciplinary procedures may follow involving periods of suspension from playing football and in some cases payment of fines.

The following examples illustrate some acts of misconduct which damage not only the individual reputations of the players concerned, but also offend the true ideals of sporting play.

Showing dissent, by word or action, from any decision given by the Referee. (Caution for first offence).

Foul play during a stoppage in tne game. (Dismissal).

Entering the field of play without the permission of the Referee. (Caution). An indirect free-kick is awarded to the opposing team.

Any action intended to distract an opponent. (Caution).

Kicking the ball away from the place where a free-kick is to be taken, to indicate dissent and to gain an unfair advantage for the offending team. (Caution).

Distracting, or attempting to distract, an opponent by shouting. (Caution). Indirect free-kick awarded to opposing team.

Interference by club officials in issuing instructions to players during the game. Players are expected to make their own decisions during play and must not receive outside assistance. (Caution to club official).

Misconduct to the Referee, at any time, even though it occurs off the field of play, will be dealt with as if it occurred during the game.

Misconduct to a Linesman at any time before, during or after the game. (Caution or dismissal according to offence).

73

Section 4

MATCH CONTROL

Match Control

Football is a game full of action and excitement. Individual and team skills are matched to provide pleasure and entertainment.

The game must be played to certain rules and it is necessary to have an independent authority to enforce these rules and to decide any disputed point. A qualified Referee is a trained expert in arbitrating in such matters and is required to interpret sensibly the basic intentions of the Laws in actual play.

The Referee is given wide powers to exercise proper control of the game and is the only practical link between the administrators and the players.

This Section outlines some of his duties and powers and the tactical method of match control adopted by the Referee and his assistants, the two Linesmen.

In some competitions the Referee is required to display a yellow card, indicating a caution, or a red card, indicating a dismissal. A green card is sometimes shown to signal permission to a trainer to enter the field to deal with an injured player.

PENCIL
NOTEBOOK

WHISTLE
ATTACHED
TO WRIST

IN POCKET:
COIN
STOPWATCH
EXTRA WHISTLE
EXTRA PENCIL
WRIST WATCH

THE REFEREE.
USUAL DRESS AND EQUIPMENT.

The Referee has power to penalise when play has been stopped. In this case a defending player strikes an opponent as a corner-kick is about to be taken. The defender would be dismissed and the game still restarted with the corner-kick because the ball was 'out of play' when the offence occurred.

If an attacking player (No. 8) is fouled but to stop play would give the offending team an advantage, possibly preventing a goal from being scored, the Referee has power to refrain from penalising and allow play to continue. He should still deal with the offending player later (i.e. with a caution or dismissal) according to the nature of the offence.

A defending player may attempt to prevent a goal being scored by deliberately handling the ball. If the ball enters goal the Referee will allow the goal and not award a penalty-kick for the handling offence. He may also caution the offending player.

The Referee has power to stop the game if, in his opinion, a player is seriously injured.

No person other than the players and Linesmen may enter the field of play without the Referee's permission. In the situation shown here, the trainer may be cautioned and reported.

Neutral Linesmen, when appointed, are drawn from a panel of qualified referees. They are required to assist the Referee to control the game in accordance with the Laws.

A Linesman reports an offence by an attacker, which he has noticed immediately prior to the scoring of a goal. The Referee, if he has not observed the incident, may act on the Linesman's advice and cancel the goal.

If the ball strikes a Linesman and is deflected over a boundary line the game shall be restarted by a throw-in, goal-kick or corner-kick. In this case it would be a corner-kick because a defending player last touched the ball and it was deflected over the goal-line.

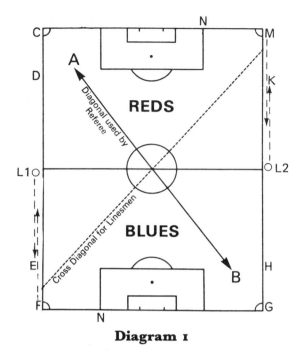

Diagram 1

The imaginary diagonal used by the Referee is the line A—B.

The opposite diagonal used by the Linesmen is adjusted to the position of the Referee; if the Referee is near A, Linesman L2 will be at a point between M and K. When the Referee is at B, Linesman L1 will be between E and F; this gives TWO officials control of the respective 'danger zones', one at each side of the field.

Linesman L1 adopts the REDS as his side; Linesman L2 adopts the BLUES; as RED forwards move toward Blue goal, Linesman L1 keeps in line with second last BLUE defender so in actual practice he will rarely get into Red's half of the field. Similarly Linesman L2 keeps in line with second last RED defender, and will rarely get into Blue's half.

At corner-kicks or penalty-kicks the Linesman in that half where the corner-kick or penalty-kick occurs positions himself at N and the Referee takes position.

The diagonal system fails if Linesman L2 gets between G and H when Referee is at B, or when Linesman L1 is near C or D when the Referee is at A, because there are TWO officials at the same place. This should be avoided.

(N.B.—Some Referees prefer to use the opposite diagonal, viz., from F to M, in which case the Linesmen should adjust their work accordingly.)

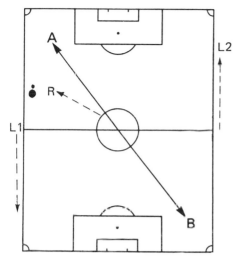

2 Development of attack

Ball moves out to left wing, Referee (R) slightly off diagonal to be near play.

Linesman (L2) level with second last defender.

Two officials, therefore, up with play.

Linesman (L1) in position for clearance and possible counter-attack.

**3 Free-kick near goal
(Just outside penalty-area)**

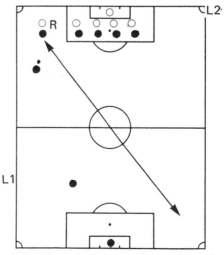

Players ● and ○ line up for free-kick.

Referee (R) takes up his position just off his diagonal so that he is placed accurately to judge off-side. Linesman (L2) is more advanced but can watch for off-side and fouls and also is in a good position to act as goal judge in the event of a direct shot being taken.

Section 5

PLAYERS CODE
PLAYERS GUIDE
REFEREES GUIDE
CLUB OFFICIALS GUIDE

PLAYERS CODE

Football, to be universally enjoyed, has to be played to a standard code of conduct.

The Spirit of the Game, as described earlier, gives a general guide as to what the legislators bear in mind when formulating the Laws.

To avoid bringing the game into disrepute players are expected to observe the following code of practice:

Decisions — Accept the decisions of the match officials without question. On points of fact these are always FINAL.

Respect — Treat opponents and officials with the respect you would wish them to accord to you.

Appeals — Avoid appealing for decisions to be given in your favour e.g. throw-ins; corner-kicks; apparent infringements by opponents.

Fair Play — Play fairly and without danger to opponents.

Discipline — Keep your temper under all circumstances.

Disputes — Support the Referee immediately should any dispute arise.

Sportsmanship — Do not indulge in practices of cheating under the guise of 'gamesmanship'.

Honour — To win without honour is a hollow victory.

PLAYERS GUIDE

A clear understanding of the Laws will improve your play and add to your enjoyment. Difficulties will be avoided if you follow the guide notes given below.

Equipment

Before every game check your equipment for any item which may prove dangerous to yourself or opponents. Boots, in particular, need careful attention.

Starting Play

Remember the ball is not in play until it has been kicked. The signal for the kick to be taken is not the signal for you to move nearer than 10 yards.

Ball Out of Play

The **whole** of the ball must pass over the boundary lines before it is out of play. The named areas include the lines which mark their boundaries.

Free-Kick Position

Free-kicks must be taken from the place where the infringement occurred.

10 Yards

Check what 10 yards means and retire to this distance immediately a free-kick is awarded against your team.

Throw-in Positions

Throw-ins must be taken from the point where the ball crossed the touch-line.

Goalkeepers

When playing as goalkeeper remember the following:—

(a) Wear colours which distinguish you from other players and the referee.

(b) You may be charged fairly—

Goalkeepers (Contd.)
    (i)   when not in possession of the ball outside your goal-area,

    (ii)   when holding the ball,

    (iii)   when obstructing an opponent.

    (c)   When you have possession of the ball release it quickly and without taking more than 4 steps. When the ball has been released you may play it with your feet, but not with your hands, until it has been played by another player.

    (d)   Avoid any tactics which may be interpreted as time-wasting e.g. excessive bouncing of the ball.

    (e)   Pulling down the crossbar to prevent the ball from entering goal is misconduct.

    (f)   Avoid distracting opponents by shouting when challenged for the ball.

    (g)   At a penalty-kick, stand still on your goal-line until the ball is kicked.

    (h)   Advise the Referee if you intend changing places with another player.

Off-side
Study the illustrations of Off-side in Section 3 and Law 11 in Section 6. Remember the following:—

    (a)   Off-side is firstly, a matter of FACT (the position of the player) and secondly, a matter of OPINION (possible influence on play or motive for being in an off-side position).

    (b)   Position is judged **at the moment the ball is played,** not where the player is when he receives it.

    (c)   You cannot be off-side if you are behind the ball or

Off-side (Contd.)   from a goal-kick, corner-kick, throw-in or dropped ball, in your own half, or when there are two or more defenders nearer the goal-line.

(d)   One of the two or more defenders does not have to be the goalkeeper.

(e)   If you are in an off-side position you can do nothing to put yourself on-side but, by keeping clear of play and opponents, you may avoid being penalised.

Foul Play   Study Law 12 in Section 3 and Section 6.

(a)   Any one of the nine major offences (a) to (i), committed intentionally (in the opinion of the Referee), will result in a direct free-kick to the opposing side. If committed in the penalty-area the award is a penalty-kick.

(b)   Try to avoid any action which may endanger other players e.g. attempting to kick the ball when the goalkeeper is holding it.

(c)   A fair charge is not allowed if the ball is not within playing distance and no attempt is being made to play the ball.

(d)   Obstruction will not be penalised if the ball is being played.

Misconduct   The latter part of Law 12 should be given careful consideration to avoid serious breaches of the Players Code. No true sportsman enjoys the spectacle of a player being officially cautioned or dismissed from the field.

Penalty-Kicks   From Law 14 note the following:—

(a)   The positions of the players.

(b)   The ball must be kicked forward.

(c)   The ball is not in play until it has been kicked.

Penalty-Kicks
(Contd.)

(d) Players must remain at the proper distances until the ball is in play. Those who do encroach will be cautioned.

(e) The examples of when a penalty-kick is considered completed after time has been extended.

Match Control

Laws 5 and 6 provide the match officials with wide powers to control play. Note particularly that the Referee need not stop play for an infringement if he considers that the offending team will gain an advantage.

REFEREES GUIDE

Your role in the playing of football is vital. The manner in which you interpret and apply the Laws of the Game can greatly influence the amount of pleasure gained by those who play or watch.

Every game poses a variety of problems requiring instant and correct decisions. Only by clearly understanding the purpose of each Law can you carry out your duties efficiently. Some problems may arise which do not have written answers. These must be solved by the application of commonsense.

A careful study of the Spirit of the Game will assist in appreciating your role as the only practical link between the legislators and players.

The following notes should be helpful in applying the Laws efficiently.

Section 1   Components

Check List

Establish a routine method of checking the components of the game by compiling a list of items to be examined. Your list should include the following:—

(a) **Field**—outside dimensions, line markings, inside areas, penalty and centre marks. Safety of playing surface.

(b) **Goals**—size, safety of construction, colour, nets.

(c) **Flag Posts**—positions, height, safety of construction.

(d) **Ball**—Shape, size, pressure, weight, safety of construction. Spare ball if available.

(e) **Players' equipment**—colours, boots, other articles which may prove dangerous.

(f) **Players**—number on each side, goalkeepers, substitutes, if permitted.

Section 2   Laws of Play

Competition Rules

Check for any additions to or variations from the Laws which have been agreed between the competing teams. In particular:—

(a) **Components**—for very young players competitors may agree to modify the size of the playing area, size, weight and material of the ball and size of goals.

(b) **Timing**—the normal period of 90 minutes may be reduced. A period of extra time may be allowable under certain conditions.

Timing	(a)	Play must be divided into **two equal** periods.
	(b)	Allowance may be made for time lost, at your discretion. It is usual practice to make allowances for delay in play due to injuries, timewasting or prolonged stoppages, but not for normal stoppages, such as throw-ins, goal-kicks, corner-kicks, etc.
	(c)	Players have a right to an interval at half-time.
Free-Kicks	(a)	Allow free-kicks to be taken as quickly as possible so that the offending team do not gain any advantage by using delay to organise their defence.
	(b)	The ball must be stationary before the kick is taken and it must travel the distance of its circumference before being played.
	(c)	Caution any player of the offending team who attempts to delay the free-kick e.g. by kicking the ball away.
	(d)	Caution any player of the offending team who refuses to retire to the proper distance from the ball before the kick is taken.
	(e)	When awarding an indirect free-kick raise one arm above your head before you give a signal, usually by whistle, for the kick to be taken.
	(f)	If a player kicks the ball direct into his own goal, from a free-kick taken outside the penalty-area, the correct decision is a corner-kick.
	(g)	If the ball goes direct into the opponents goal from an indirect free-kick the correct decision is a goal-kick.
Goals	(a)	A goal cannot be awarded if the whole of the ball does not cross the goal-line between the posts and under the cross-bar.

93

Goals (Contd.)

(b) Before awarding a goal be sure that your linesmen, if neutral, are not trying to bring to your notice an incident which you may have missed. A goal cannot be cancelled after play has been restarted.

(c) Keep a record of the goals as they are scored.

Section 3   **Off-side and Foul Play**

Off-Side

(a) Decide immediately if a player in an off-side position is interfering with play, opponents, or is trying to gain an advantage before stopping play.

(b) The positions of players relative to off-side apply only at the moment the ball is played.

Fouls

(a) Study carefully the illustrations of major offences for which a direct free-kick is awarded.

(b) You must satisfy yourself that the offence was **intentional** before awarding a free-kick.

(c) Watch closely for unfair charging on the goalkeeper. Also for any dangerous play from opponents attempting to kick the ball while being held by him.

Misconduct

(a) Deal promptly and firmly with any player who persistently infringes the Laws or who argues with your decision.

(b) Watch carefully for any attempt by players to provoke opponents into retaliatory actions.

(c) Players who continue misconduct after receiving a caution must be dismissed from the game.

Misconduct (Contd.)   (d)   A timely word of advice to players who appear to be losing self-control may help to complete the game without the necessity for severe disciplinary action.

(e)   All cases of misconduct must be reported to the appropriate authority.

Section 4   **Match Control**

Advantage   (a)   Note that you need not stop play for an infringement if the offending side would gain an advantage.

(b)   To apply the advantage clause does not preclude you from taking disciplinary action against the offending player.

Injured Players   (a)   Stop the game only if you consider that a player has been seriously injured. Arrange for him to be taken off the field for attention and restart play promptly.

(b)   Where players are slightly injured wait for a normal stoppage in play and allow him to be treated, off the field if possible.

(c)   Some players may pretend to be injured to gain an advantage i.e. a free-kick, to waste time or even to get an opponent into trouble. Be alert to these actions.

(d)   If you consider an injury has been caused by defective boot studs, you have power to inspect boots and send any offending players from the field for the defects to be corrected.

Illegal Coaching   When the game is in progress players must make their own decisions. Prevent any attempt by club officials to coach from the boundary lines.

95

Illegal Entry	Do not allow trainers or other persons to enter the field of play without your permission.
Match Control	Study the application of the Diagonal System of Control. Establish clearly any special points to be observed by linesmen.
Signals	With the exception of the use of the whistle and raising one arm to indicate an indirect free-kick, the Laws do not specify any special code of signals. Referees are advised to communicate decisions clearly without undue demonstration.

CLUB OFFICIALS GUIDE

Many clubs enter teams in competitions. They agree to play to the rules of these competitions in addition to the Laws of the Game.

The officials of each club should understand what is expected of them to preserve the good name of their club, competition and of the Game.

The following notes outline the main responsibilities and duties of Club Officials.

Every club is responsible for the conduct of its players and officials.

Club Secretaries are responsible for ensuring that players and competitions in which the club takes part are properly registered and approved by the appropriate authority.

Clubs in charge of the arrangements for any match are responsible for the welfare of the match officials before, during and after the match. In certain circumstances competitions or governing authorities may undertake this responsibility.

The club in charge of match arrangements is responsible for the following:—

(a) Proper marking of the field of play.

(b) Providing correct equipment e.g. goals, nets where possible, corner flags and posts, linesmen's flags and match ball.

(c) Size of playing area conforming with the Laws of the Game and any special rules of a competition.

(d) Advising appointed match officials of full details relating to place where the match is to be played, time of kick-off and any other relevant information.

(e) Providing suitable dressing facilities for players and match officials.

(f) Whenever possible, providing a suitable barrier between the playing area and spectators. Sufficient space to be allowed to avoid interference with play and danger from collision by players.

Trainers, Coaches and other Club Officials should be instructed not to enter the field of play while a game is in progress, without the permission of the Referee.

Clubs should take action to exclude from any match all persons known to have committed misconduct towards match officials.

Section 6

LAWS
OF
ASSOCIATION FOOTBALL

INDEX

Notes

Provided the principles of these Laws be maintained they may be modified in their application :—

1. To players of school age as follows :
   (a) size of playing pitch;
   (b) size, weight and material of ball;
   (c) width between the goal-posts and height of the cross-bar from the ground;
   (d) the duration of the periods of play;
   (e) number of substitutions.

2. For matches played by women as follows :
   (a) size, weight and material of ball;
   (b) duration of the periods of play;
   (c) further modifications are only permissible with the consent of The International Football Association Board.

LAW 1

THE FIELD OF PLAY

The Field of Play and appurtenances shall be as shown in the following plan:

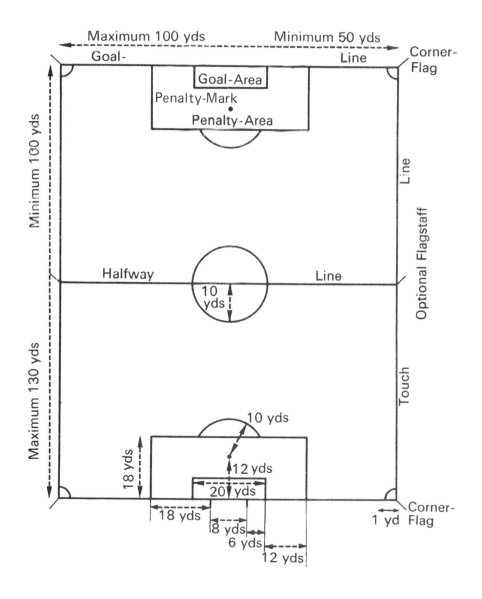

(1) **Dimensions.** The field of play shall be rectangular, its length being not more than 130 yards nor less than 100 yards and its breadth not more than 100 yards nor less than 50 yards. (In International Matches the length shall be not more than 120 yards nor less than 110 yards and the breadth not more than 80 yards nor less than 70 yards.) The length shall in all cases exceed the breadth.

(2) **Marking.** The field of play shall be marked with distinctive lines, not more than 5 inches in width, not by a V-shaped rut, in accordance with the plan, the longer boundary lines being called the touch-lines and the shorter the goal-lines. A flag on a post not less than 5 feet high and having a non-pointed top, shall be placed at each corner; a similar flag-post may be placed opposite the halfway-line on each side of the field of play, not less than 1 yard outside the touch-line. A halfway-line shall be marked out across the field of play. The centre of the field of play shall be indicated by a suitable mark and a circle with a 10 yards radius shall be marked round it.

(3) **The Goal-Area.** At each end of the field of play two lines shall be drawn at right-angles to the goal-line, 6 yards from each goal-post. These shall extend into the field of play for a distance of 6 yards and shall be joined by a line drawn parallel with the goal-line. Each of the spaces enclosed by these lines and the goal-line shall be called a goal-area.

(4) **The Penalty-Area.** At each end of the field of play two lines shall be drawn at right-angles to the goal-line, 18 yards from each goal-post. These shall extend into the field of play for a distance of 18 yards and shall be joined by a line drawn parallel with the goal-line. Each of the spaces enclosed by these lines and the goal-line shall be called a penalty-area. A suitable mark shall be made within each penalty-area, 12 yards from the mid-point of the goal-line, measured along an undrawn line at right angles thereto. These shall be the penalty-kick marks. From each penalty-kick mark an arc of a circle, having a radius of 10 yards, shall be drawn outside the penalty-area.

(5) **The Corner-Area.** From each corner-flag post a quarter circle, having a radius of 1 yard, shall be drawn inside the field of play.

(6) **The Goals.** The Goals shall be placed on the centre of each goal-line and shall consist of two upright posts, equidistant from the corner-flags and 8 yards apart (inside measurement), joined by a horizontal cross-bar the lower edge of which shall be 8 ft. from the ground. The width and depth of the goal-posts and the width and depth of the cross-bars shall not exceed 5 inches (12 cm). The goal-posts and the cross-bars shall have the same width.

Nets may be attached to the posts, cross-bars and ground behind the goals. They should be appropriately supported and be so placed as to allow the goalkeeper ample room.

INTERNATIONAL BOARD DECISIONS

1. In International matches the dimensions of the field of play shall be: maximum 110 metres × 75 metres; minimum 100 metres × 64 metres.

2. National Associations must adhere strictly to these dimensions. Each National Association organising an International Match must advise the visiting Association, before the match, of the place and the dimensions of the field of play.

3. The Board has approved this table of measurements for the Laws of the Game,

			Metres				*Metres*
130 yards	..	..	120	8 feet	..	..	2·44
120 yards	..	..	110	5 feet	..	..	1·50
110 yards	..	..	100	28 inches	..	..	0·71
100 yards	..	..	90	27 inches	..	..	0·68
80 yards	..	..	75	9 inches	..	..	0·22
70 yards	..	..	64	5 inches	..	..	0·12
50 yards	..	..	45	¾ inch	..	..	0·019
18 yards	..	..	16·50	½ inch	..	..	0·0127
12 yards	..	..	11	⅜ inch	..	..	0·010
10 yards	..	..	9·15	14 ozs.	..	..	396 grams
8 yards	..	..	7·32	16 ozs.	..	..	453 grams
6 yards	..	..	5·50	8.5 lb./sq.in.	..	600 g/cm²
1 yard	..	..	1	15·6 lb./sq.in.	..	1·100 kg/cm²

4. The goal-line shall be marked the same width as the depth of the goal-posts and the cross-bar so that the goal-line and the goal-posts will conform to the same interior and exterior edges.

5. The 6 yards (for the outline of the goal-area) and the 18 yards (for the outline of the penalty-area) which have to be measured along the goal-line, must start from the inner sides of the goal-posts.

6. The space within the inside areas of the field of play includes the width of the lines marking these areas.

7. All Associations shall provide standard equipment, particularly in International Matches, when the Laws of the Game must be complied with in every respect and especially with regard to the size of the ball and other equipment which must conform to the regulations. All cases of failure to provide standard equipment must be reported to F.I.F.A.

8. In a match played under the rules of a competition if the cross-bar becomes displaced or broken play shall be stopped and the match abandoned unless the cross-bar has been repaired and replaced in position or a new one provided without such being a danger to the players. A rope is not considered a satisfactory substitute for a cross-bar.

In a friendly match, by mutual consent, play may be resumed without the cross-bar provided it has been removed and no longer constitutes a danger to the players. In these circumstances, a rope may be used as a substitute for a cross-bar. If a rope is not used and the ball crosses the goal-line at a point which in the opinion of the Referee is below where the cross-bar should have been he shall award a goal.

The game shall be restarted by the Referee dropping the ball at the place where it was when play was stopped, unless it was within the goal area at that time, in which case it shall be dropped on that part of the goal area line which runs parallel to the goal-line, at the point nearest to where the ball was when play was stopped.

9. National Associations may specify such maximum and minimum dimensions for the cross-bars and goal-posts, within the limits laid down in Law 1, as they consider appropriate.

10. Goal-posts and cross-bars must be made of wood, metal or other approved material as decided from time to time by the International F.A. Board. They may be square, rectangular, round, half round, or elliptical in shape. Goal-posts and cross-bars made of other materials and in other shapes are not permitted.

11. 'Curtain-raisers' to International matches should only be played following agreement on the day of the match, and taking into account the condition of the field of play, between representatives of the two Associations and the referee (of the International match).

12. National Associations, particularly in International matches, should
- restrict the number of photographers around the field of play.
- have a line ('photographers' line') marked behind the goal-lines at least two metres from the corner-flag going through a point situated at least 3.5 metres behind the intersection of the goal-line with the line marking the goal area to a point situated at

least six metres behind the goal-posts.
- prohibit photographers from passing over these lines.
- forbid the use of artificial lighting in the form of 'flash-lights'.

LAW 2

THE BALL

The ball shall be spherical; the outer casing shall be of leather or other approved materials. No material shall be used in its construction which might prove dangerous to the players.

The circumference of the ball shall not be more than 28 inches and not less than 27 inches. The weight of the ball at the start of the game shall not be more than 16 oz, nor less than 14 oz. The pressure shall be equal to 0.6—1.1 atmosphere (600 – 1,100 gr/cm^2) at sea level. The ball shall not be changed during the game unless authorised by the Referee.

INTERNATIONAL BOARD DECISIONS

1. The ball used in any match shall be considered the property of the Association or Club on whose ground the match is played, and at the close of play it must be returned to the referee.

2. The International Board, from time to time, shall decide what constitutes approved materials. Any approved material shall be certified as such by the International Board.

3. The Board has approved these equivalents of the weights specified in the Law:

14 to 16 ounces = 396 to 453 grammes.

4. If the ball bursts or becomes deflated during the course of a match, the game shall be stopped and restarted by dropping the new ball at the place where the first ball became defective, unless it was within the goal area at that time, in which case it shall be dropped on that part of the goal area line which runs parallel to the goal line, at the point nearest to where the ball was when play was stopped.

5. If this happens during a stoppage of the game (place-kick, goal-kick, corner-kick, free-kick, penalty-kick or throw-in) the game shall be restarted accordingly.

LAW 3

NUMBER OF PLAYERS

(1) A match shall be played by two teams, each consisting of not more than eleven players, one of whom shall be the goalkeeper.

(2) Substitutes may be used in any match played under the rules of an official competition at FIFA. Confederation or National Association level, subject to the following conditions:

(*a*) that the authority of the international association(s) or national association(s) concerned, has been obtained,

(*b*) that, subject to the restriction contained in the following paragraph (*c*) the rules of a competition shall state how many, if any, substitutes may be used, and

(*c*) that a team shall not be permitted to use more than two substitutes in any match who must be chosen from not more than five players whose names shall be given to the Referee prior to the commencement of the match.

(3) Substitutes may be used in any other match, provided that the two teams concerned reach agreement on a maximum number, not exceeding five, and that the terms of such agreement are intimated to the Referee, before the match. If the Referee is not informed, or if the teams fail to reach agreement, no more than two substitutes shall be permitted. In all cases the substitutes must be chosen from not more than five players whose names shall be given to the Referee prior to the commencement of the match.

(4) Any of the other players may change places with the goalkeeper, provided that the Referee is informed before the change is made, and provided also, that the change is made during a stoppage of the game.

(5) When a goalkeeper or any other player is to be replaced by a substitute, the following conditions shall be observed:

(*a*) the Referee shall be informed of the proposed substitution, before it is made,

(*b*) the substitute shall not enter the field of play until the player he is replacing has left, and then only after having received a signal from the Referee,

(*c*) he shall enter the field during a stoppage in the game, and at the half-way line.

(*d*) A player who has been replaced shall not take any further part in the game.

(*e*) A substitute shall be subject to the authority and jurisdiction of the Referee whether called upon to play or not.

(*f*) The substitution is completed when the substitute enters the field of play, from which moment he becomes a player and the player whom he is replacing ceases to be a player.

Punishment:

(*a*) Play shall not be stopped for an infringement of paragraph 4. The players concerned shall be cautioned immediately the ball goes out of play.

(*b*) If a substitute enters the field of play without the authority of the Referee, play shall be stopped. The substitute shall be cautioned and removed from the field or sent off according to the circumstances. The game shall be restarted by the Referee dropping the ball at the place where it was when play was stopped, unless it was within the goal area at that time, in which case it shall be dropped on that part of the goal area line which runs parallel to the goal line, at the point nearest to where the ball was when play was stopped.

(*c*) For any other infringement of this law, the player concerned shall be cautioned, and if the game is stopped by the Referee, to administer the caution, it shall be re-started by an indirect free-kick, to be taken by a player of the opposing team, from the place where the ball was, when play was stopped, subject to the over-riding conditions imposed in Law 13.

INTERNATIONAL BOARD DECISIONS

1. The minimum number of players in a team is left to the discretion of National Associations.

2. The Board is of the opinion that a match should not be considered valid if there are fewer than seven players in either of the teams.

3. A player who has been ordered off before play begins may only be replaced by one of the named substitutes. The kick-off must not be delayed to allow the substitute to join his team.

A player who has been ordered off after play has started may not be replaced.

A named substitute who has been ordered off, either before or after play has started, may not be replaced. (This decision only relates to players who are ordered off under Law 13. It does not apply to players who have infringed Law 4.)

LAW 4

PLAYERS' EQUIPMENT

A player shall not wear anything which is dangerous to another player. Footwear (boots or shoes) must conform to the following standard:—

(a) Bars shall be made of leather or rubber and shall be transverse and flat, not less than half an inch in width and shall extend the total width of the sole and be rounded at the corners.

(b) Studs which are independently mounted on the sole and are replaceable shall be made of leather, rubber, aluminium, plastic or similar material and shall be solid. With the exception of that part of the stud forming the base, which shall not protrude from the sole more than one-quarter of an inch, studs shall be round in plan and not less than half an inch in diameter. Where studs are tapered, the minimum diameter of any section of the stud must not be less than half an inch. Where metal seating for the screw type is used, this seating must be embedded in the sole of the footwear and any attachment screw shall be part of the stud. Other than the metal seating for the screw type of stud, no metal plates even though covered with leather or rubber shall be worn, neither studs which are threaded to allow them to be screwed on to a base screw that is fixed by nails or otherwise to the soles of footwear, nor studs which, apart from the base, have any form of protruding edge rim, or relief marking, or ornament, should be allowed.

(c) Studs which are moulded as an integral part of the sole and are not replaceable shall be made of rubber, plastic, polyurethane or similar soft materials. Provided that there are no fewer than ten studs on the sole, they shall have a minimum diameter of three-eighths of an inch (10 mm). Additional supporting material to stabilise studs of soft materials, and ridges which shall not protrude more than 5 mm from the sole and moulded to strengthen it, shall be permitted provided that they are in no way dangerous to other players. In all other respects they shall conform to the general requirements of this law.

(d) Combined bars and studs may be worn, provided the whole conforms to the general requirements of this law. Neither bars nor studs on the soles shall project more than three-quarters of an inch. If nails are used they shall be driven in flush with the surface.

The goalkeeper shall wear colours which distinguish him from the other players and from the Referee.

Punishment. For any infringement of this Law, the player at fault shall be sent off the field of play to adjust his equipment and he shall not return without first reporting to the Referee, who shall satisfy himself that the player's equipment is in order; the player shall only re-enter the game at a moment when the ball has ceased to be in play.

INTERNATIONAL BOARD DECISIONS

1. The usual equipment of a player is a jersey or shirt, shorts, stockings and footwear. In a match played under the rules of a competition, players need not wear boots or shoes, but shall wear jersey or shirt, shorts, or track suit or similar trousers, and stockings.

2. The Law does not insist that boots or shoes must be worn. However, in competition matches Referees should not allow one or a few players to play without footwear when all the other players are so equipped.

3. In International Matches, International Competitions, International Club Competitions and friendly matches between clubs of different National Associations, the Referee, prior to the start of the match, shall inspect the players' footwear and prevent any player whose footwear does not conform to the requirements of this law from playing until such times as it does comply. The rules of any competition may include a similar provision.

4. If the Referee finds that a player is wearing articles not permitted by the Laws and which may constitute a danger to other players, he shall order him to take them off. If he fails to carry out the Referee's instruction, the player shall not take part in the match.

5. A Player who has been prevented from taking part in the game or a player who has been sent off the field for infringing Law 4 must report to the Referee during a stoppage of the game and may not enter or re-enter the field of play unless and until the Referee has satisfied himself that the player is no longer infringing Law 4.

6. A player who has been prevented from taking part in a game or who has been sent off because of an infringement of Law 4, and who enters or re-enters the field of play to join or rejoin his team, in breach of the conditions of Law 12, shall be cautioned.

If the Referee stops the game to administer the caution, the game shall be restarted by an indirect free-kick, taken by a player of the opposing side, from the place where the ball was when the Referee stopped the game, subject to the over-riding conditions imposed in Law 13.

LAW 5

REFEREES

A Referee shall be appointed to officiate in each game. His authority and the exercise of the powers granted to him by the Laws of the Game commence as soon as he enters the field of play.

His power of penalizing shall extend to offences committed when play has been temporarily suspended, or when the ball is out of play. His decision on points of fact connected with the play shall be final, so far as the result of the game is concerned.

He shall:—

(a) Enforce the Laws.

(b) Refrain from penalizing in cases where he is satisfied that, by doing so, he would be giving an advantage to the offending team.

(c) Keep a record of the game; act as timekeeper and allow the full or agreed time, adding thereto all time lost through accident or other cause.

(d) Have discretionary power to stop the game for any infringement of the Laws and to suspend or terminate the game whenever, by reason of the elements, interference by spectators, or other cause, he deems such stoppage necessary. In such a case he shall submit a detailed report to the competent authority, within the stipulated time, and in accordance with the provisions set up by the National Association under whose jurisdiction the match was played. Reports will be deemed to be made when received in the ordinary course of post.

(e) From the time he enters the field of play, caution any player guilty of misconduct or ungentlemanly behaviour and, if he persists, to suspend him from further participation in the game. In such cases the Referee shall send the name of the offender to the competent authority, within the stipulated time, and in accordance with the provisions set up by the National Association under whose jurisdiction the match was played. Reports will be deemed to be made when received in the ordinary course of post.

(f) Allow no person other than the players and Linesmen to enter the field of play without his permission.

(g) Stop the game if, in his opinion, a player has been seriously injured; have the player removed as soon as possible from the field of play, and immediately resume the game. If a player is slightly injured, the game shall not be stopped until the ball has ceased to be in play. A player who is able to go to the touch- or goal-line for attention of any kind, shall not be treated on the field of play.

(*h*) Send off the field of play, any player who, in his opinion, is guilty of violent conduct, serious foul play, or the use of foul or abusive language.

(*i*) Signal for recommencement of the game after all stoppages.

(*j*) Decide that the ball provided for a match meets with the requirements of Law 2.

INTERNATIONAL BOARD DECISIONS

1. Referees in International Matches shall wear a blazer or blouse the colour of which is distinctive from the colours worn by the contesting teams.

2. Referees for International Matches will be selected from a neutral country unless the countries concerned agree to appoint their own officials.

3. The Referee must be chosen from the official list of International Referees. This need not apply to Amateur and Youth International matches.

4. The Referee shall report to the appropriate authority misconduct or any misdemeanour on the part of spectators, officials, players, named substitutes or other persons which take place either on the field of play or in its vicinity at any time prior to, during, or after the match in question so that appropriate action can be taken by the Authority concerned.

5. Linesmen are assistants of the Referee. In no case shall the Referee consider the intervention of a Linesman if he himself has seen the incident and from his position on the field, is better able to judge. With this reserve, and the Linesman neutral, the Referee can consider the intervention and if the information of the Linesman applies to that phase of the game immediately before the scoring of a goal, the Referee may act thereon and cancel the goal.

6. The Referee, however, can only reverse his first decision so long as the game has not been restarted.

7. If the Referee has decided to apply the advantage clause and to let the game proceed, he cannot revoke his decision if the presumed advantage has not been realised, even though he has not, by any gesture, indicated his decision. This does not exempt the offending player from being dealt with by the Referee.

8. The Laws of the Game are intended to provide that games should be played with as little interference as possible, and in this view it is the duty of Referees to penalise only deliberate breaches of the Law. Constant whistling for trifling and doubtful breaches produces bad feeling and loss of temper on the part of the players and spoils the pleasure of spectators.

9. By para. (*d*) of Law 5 the Referee is empowered to terminate a match in the event of grave disorder, but he has no power or right to decide, in such event, that either team is disqualified and thereby the loser of the match. He must send a detailed report to the proper authority who alone has power to deal further with this matter.

10. If a player commits two infringements of a different nature at the same time, the Referee shall punish the more serious offence.

11. It is the duty of the Referee to act upon the information of neutral Linesmen with regard to incidents that do not come under the personal notice of the Referee.

12. The Referee shall not allow any person to enter the field until play has stopped, and only then, if he has given him a signal to do so, nor shall he allow coaching from the boundary lines.

LAW 6

LINESMEN

Two Linesmen shall be appointed, whose duty (subject to the decision of the Referee) shall be to indicate:
    (*a*) when the ball is out of play,
    (*b*) which side is entitled to a corner-kick, goal-kick or throw-in,
    (*c*) when a substitution is desired.

They shall also assist the Referee to control the game in accordance with the Laws. In the event of undue interference or improper conduct by a Linesman, the Referee shall dispense with his services and arrange for a substitute to be appointed. (The matter shall be reported by the Referee to the competent authority.) The Linesmen should be equipped with flags by the Club on whose ground the match is played.

INTERNATIONAL BOARD DECISIONS

1. Linesmen where neutral shall draw the Referee's attention to any breach of the Laws of the Game of which they become aware if they consider that the Referee may not have seen it, but the Referee shall always be the judge of the decision to be taken.

2. National Associations are advised to appoint official Referees of neutral nationality to act as Linesmen in International Matches.

3. In International Matches, Linesmens' flags shall be of a vivid colour—bright reds and yellows. Such flags are recommended for use in all other matches.

4. A Linesman may be subject to disciplinary action only upon a report of the Referee for unjustified interference or insufficient assistance.

LAW 7

DURATION OF THE GAME

The duration of the game shall be two equal periods of 45 minutes, unless otherwise mutually agreed upon, subject to the following:—

(*a*) Allowance shall be made in either period for all time lost through substitution, the transport from the field of injured players, time-wasting or other cause, the amount of which shall be a matter for the discretion of the Referee;

(*b*) Time shall be extended to permit of a penalty-kick being taken at or after the expiration of the normal period in either half.

At half-time the interval shall not exceed five minutes except by consent of the **Referee.**

1. If a match has been stopped by the Referee, before the completion of the time specified in the rules, for any reason stated in Law 5 it must be replayed in full unless the rules of the competition concerned provide for the result of the match at the time of such stoppage to stand.

2. Players have a right to an interval at half-time.

LAW 8

THE START OF PLAY

(*a*) **At the beginning of the game,** choice of ends and the kick-off shall be decided by the toss of a coin. The team winning the toss shall have the option of choice of ends or the kick-off.

The Referee, having given a signal, the game shall be started by a player taking a place-kick (i.e., a kick at the ball while it is stationary on the ground in the centre of the field of play) into his opponents' half of the field of play. Every player shall be in his own half of the field and every player of the team opposing that of the kicker shall remain not less than 10 yards from the ball until it is kicked-off; it shall not be deemed in play until it has travelled the distance of its own circumference. The kicker shall not play the ball a second time until it has been touched or played by another player.

(*b*) **After a goal has been scored,** the game shall be restarted in like manner by a player of the team losing the goal.

(*c*) **After half-time;** when restarting after half-time, ends shall be changed and the kick-off shall be taken by a player of the opposite team to that of the player who started the game.

Punishment. For any infringement of this Law, the kick-off shall be retaken, except in the case of the kicker playing the ball again before it has been touched or played by another player; for this offence, an indirect free-kick shall be taken by a player of the opposing team from the place where the infringement occurred, subject to the over-riding conditions imposed in Law 13.

A goal shall not be scored direct from a kick-off.

(*d*) **After any other temporary suspension;** when restarting the game after a temporary suspension of play from any cause not mentioned elsewhere in these Laws, provided that immediately prior to the suspension the ball has not passed over the touch or goal-lines, the Referee shall drop the ball at the place where it was when play was suspended unless it was within the goal area at that time, in which case it shall be dropped on that part of the goal area line which runs parallel to the goal-line, at the point nearest to where the ball was when play was stopped. It shall be deemed in play when it has touched the ground; if, however, it goes over the touch- or goal-lines after it has been dropped by the Referee, but before it is touched by a player, the Referee shall again drop it. A player shall not play the ball until it has touched the ground. If this section of the Law is not complied with the Referee shall again drop the ball.

INTERNATIONAL BOARD DECISIONS

1. If, when the Referee drops the ball, a player infringes any of the Laws before the ball has touched the ground, the player concerned shall be cautioned or sent off the field according to the seriousness of the offence, but a free-kick cannot be awarded to the opposing team because the ball was not in play at the time of the offence. The ball shall therefore be again dropped by the Referee.

2. Kicking-off by persons other than the players competing in a match is prohibited.

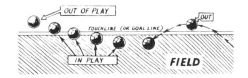

LAW 9

BALL IN AND OUT OF PLAY

The ball is out of play:—
- (*a*) When it has wholly crossed the goal-line or touch-line, whether on the **ground** or in the air.
- (*b*) When the game has been stopped by the Referee.

The ball is in play at all other times from the start of the match to the finish including:—

(*a*)   If it rebounds from a goal-post, cross-bar or corner-flag post into the field of play.

(*b*)   If it rebounds off either the Referee or Linesmen when they are in the field of play.

(*c*)   In the event of a supposed infringement of the Laws, until a decision is given.

INTERNATIONAL BOARD DECISIONS

1.   The lines belong to the areas of which they are the boundaries. In consequence, the touch-lines and the goal-lines belong to the field of play.

LAW 10

METHOD OF SCORING

Except as otherwise provided by these Laws, a goal is scored when the whole of the ball has passed over the goal-line, between the goal-posts and under the cross-bar, provided it has not been thrown, carried or intentionally propelled by hand or arm, by a player of the attacking side, except in the case of a goalkeeper, who is within his own penalty-area.

The team scoring the greater number of goals during a game shall be the winner; if no goals, or an equal number of goals are scored, the game shall be termed a "draw".

INTERNATIONAL BOARD DECISIONS

1.   Law 10 defines the only method according to which a match is won or drawn; no variation whatsoever can be authorised.

2.   A goal cannot in any case be allowed if the ball has been prevented by some outside agency from passing over the goal-line. If this happens in the normal course of play, other than at the taking of a penalty-kick, the game must be stopped and restarted by the Referee dropping the ball at the place where the ball came into contact with the interference, unless it was within the goal area at that time, in which case it shall be dropped on that part of the goal area line which runs parallel to the goal line, at the point nearest to where the ball was when play was stopped.

3. If, when the ball is going into goal, a spectator enters the field before it passes wholly over the goal-line, and tries to prevent a score, a goal shall be allowed if the ball goes into goal, unless the spectator has made contact with the ball or has interfered with play, in which case the Referee shall stop the game and restart it by dropping the ball at the place where the contact or interference occurred, unless it was within the goal area at that time, in which case it shall be dropped on that part of the goal area line which runs parallel to the goal line, at the point nearest to where the ball was when play was stopped.

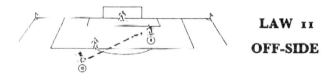

LAW 11

OFF-SIDE

1. A player is in an off-side position if he is nearer to his opponents' goal-line than the ball, unless:—
    (*a*) he is in his own half of the field of play, or
    (*b*) there are at least two of his opponents nearer their own goal-line than he is.

2. A player shall only be declared off-side and penalised for being in an off-side position, if, at the moment the ball touches, or is played by, one of his team, he is, in the opinion of the Referee
    (*a*) interfering with play or with an opponent, or
    (*b*) seeking to gain an advantage by being in that position.

3. A player shall not be declared off-side by the Referee
    (*a*) merely because of his being in an off-side position, or
    (*b*) if he receives the ball, direct, from a goal-kick, a corner-kick, a throw-in, or when it has been dropped by the Referee.

4. If a player is declared off-side, the Referee shall award an indirect free-kick, which shall be taken by a player of the opposing team from the place where the infringement occurred, unless the offence is committed by a player in his opponents' goal area, in which case, the free-kick shall be taken from a point anywhere within that half of the goal area in which the offence occurred.

117

1. Off-side shall not be judged at the moment the player in question receives the ball, but at the moment when the ball is passed to him by one of his own side. A player who is not in an off-side position when one of his colleagues passes the ball to him or takes a free-kick, does not therefore become off-side if he goes forward during the flight of the ball.

LAW 12

FOULS AND MISCONDUCT

A player who intentionally commits any of the following nine offences:—

- (a) Kicks or attempts to kick an opponent;
- (b) Trips an opponent, i.e., throwing or attempting to throw him by the use of the legs or by stooping in front of or behind him;
- (c) Jumps at an opponent;
- (d) Charges an opponent in a violent or dangerous manner;
- (e) Charges an opponent from behind unless the latter be obstructing;
- (f) Strikes or attempts to strike an opponent or spits at him;
- (g) Holds an opponent;
- (h) Pushes an opponent;
- (i) Handles the ball, i.e., carries, strikes or propels the ball with his hand or arm. (This does not apply to the goalkeeper within his own penalty-area);

shall be penalised by the award of a **direct free-kick** to be taken by the opposing team from the place where the offence occurred, unless the offence is committed by a player in his opponents' goal area, in which case, the free-kick shall be taken from a point anywhere within that half of the goal area in which the offence occurred.

Should a player of the defending side intentionally commit one of the above nine offences within the penalty-area he shall be penalised by a **penalty-kick.**

A penalty-kick can be awarded irrespective of the position of the ball, if in play, at the time an offence within the penalty-area is committed.

A player committing any of the five following offences:—

1. Playing in a manner considered by the Referee to be dangerous, e.g., attempting to kick the ball while held by the goalkeeper;

2. Charging fairly, i.e., with the shoulder, when the ball is not within playing distance of the players concerned and they are definitely not trying to play it;

3. When not playing the ball, intentionally obstructing an opponent, i.e., running between the opponent and the ball, or interposing the body so as to form an obstacle to an opponent;

4. Charging the goalkeeper except when he—
   (a) is holding the ball;
   (b) is obstructing an opponent;
   (c) has passed outside his goal-area;

5. When playing as a goalkeeper and within his own penalty-area:
   (a) from the moment he takes control of the ball with his hands, he takes more than 4 steps in any direction whilst holding, bouncing or throwing the ball in the air and catching it again, without releasing it into play, or, having released it into play before, during or after the 4 steps, he touches it again with his hands, before it has been touched or played by another player of the same team outside of the penalty area, or by a player of the opposing team either inside or outside of the penalty area,
   (b) indulges in tactics which, in the opinion of the Referee, are designed merely to hold up the game and thus waste time and so give an unfair advantage to his own team.

shall be penalised by the award of an **indirect free-kick** to be taken by the opposing team from the place where the infringement occurred, subject to the over-riding conditions imposed in Law 13.

A player shall be **cautioned** if:—
   (j) he enters or re-enters the field of play to join or re-join his team after the game has commenced, or leaves the field of play during the progress of the game (except through accident) without, in either case, first having received a signal from the Referee showing him that he may do so. If the Referee stops the game to administer the caution the game shall be restarted by an indirect free-kick taken by a player of the opposing team from the place where the ball was when the Referee stopped the game subject to the over-riding conditions imposed in Law 13.

If, however, the offending player has committed a more serious offence he shall be penalised according to that section of the law he infringed.

(*k*) he persistently infringes the Laws of the Game;

(*l*) he shows by word or action, dissent from any decision given by the Referee;

(*m*) he is guilty of ungentlemanly conduct.

For any of these last three offences, in addition to the caution, an **indirect free-kick** shall also be awarded to the opposing team from the place where the offence occurred, subject to the over-riding conditions imposed in Law 13, unless a more serious infringement of the Laws of the Game was committed.

A player shall be **sent off** the field of play, if in the opinion of the Referee, he:—

(n) is guilty of violent conduct or serious foul play;

(o) uses foul or abusive language;

(p) persists in misconduct after having received a caution.

If play be stopped by reason of a player being ordered from the field for an offence without a separate breach of the Law having been committed, the game shall be resumed by an **indirect free-kick** awarded to the opposing team from the place where the infringement occurred, subject to the over-riding conditions imposed in Law 13.

INTERNATIONAL BOARD DECISIONS

1. If the goalkeeper either intentionally strikes an opponent by throwing the ball vigorously at him, or pushes him with the ball while holding it, the Referee shall award a penalty-kick, if the offence took place within the penalty-area.

2. If a player deliberately turns his back to an opponent when he is about to be tackled, he may be charged but not in a dangerous manner.

3. In case of body-contact in the goal-area between an attacking player and the opposing goalkeeper not in possession of the ball, the Referee, as sole judge of intention, shall stop the game if, in his opinion, the action of the attacking player was intentional, and award an indirect free-kick.

4. If a player leans on the shoulders of another player of his own team in order to head the ball, the Referee shall stop the game, caution the player for ungentlemanly conduct and award an indirect free-kick to the opposing side.

5. A player's obligation when joining or rejoining his team after the start of the match to "report to the Referee" must be interpreted as meaning to "draw the attention of the Referee from the touch-line". The signal from the Referee shall be made by a definite gesture which makes the player understand that he may come into the field of play; it is not necessary for the Referee to wait until the game is stopped (This does not apply in respect of an infringement of Law 4), but the Referee is the sole judge of the moment in which he gives his signal of acknowledgement.

6. The letter and spirit of Law 12 do not oblige the Referee to stop a game to administer a caution. He may, if he chooses, apply the advantage. If he does apply the advantage, he shall caution the player when play stops.

7. If a player covers up the ball without touching it in an endeavour not to have it played by an opponent, he obstructs but does not infringe Law 12, para. 3, because he is already in possession of the ball and covers it for tactical reasons whilst the ball remains within playing distance. In fact, he is actually playing the ball and does not commit an infringement; in this case, the player may be charged because he is in fact playing the ball.

8. If a player intentionally stretches his arms to obstruct an opponent and steps from one side to the other, moving his arms up and down to delay his opponent, forcing him to change course, but does not make "bodily contact" the Referee shall caution the player for ungentlemanly conduct and award an indirect free-kick.

9. If a player intentionally obstructs the opposing goalkeeper, in an attempt to prevent him from putting the ball into play in accordance with Law 12, 5(a), the Referee shall award an indirect free-kick.

10. If after a Referee has awarded a free-kick a player protests violently by using abusive or foul language and is sent off the field, the free-kick should not be taken until the player has left the field.

11. Any player, whether he is within or outside the field of play, whose conduct is ungentlemanly or violent, whether or not it is directed towards an opponent, a colleague, the Referee, a linesman or other person, or who uses foul or abusive language, is guilty of an offence, and shall be dealt with according to the nature of the offence committed.

12.   If in the opinion of the Referee a goalkeeper intentionally lies on the ball longer than is necessary, he shall be penalised for ungentlemanly conduct and

(*a*)   be cautioned, and an indirect free-kick awarded to the opposing team;

(*b*)   In case of repetition of the offence, be sent off the field.

13.   The offence of spitting at officials or other persons, or similar unseemly behaviour, shall be considered as violent conduct within the meaning of section (n) of Law 12.

14.   If, when a Referee is about to caution a player, and before he has done so, the player commits another offence which merits a caution, the player shall be sent off the field of play.

LAW 13

FREE-KICK

Free-kicks shall be classified under two heads: "Direct" (from which a goal can be scored direct against the **offending side**), and "Indirect" (from which a goal cannot be scored unless the ball has been played or touched by a player other than the kicker before passing through the goal).

When a player is taking a direct or an indirect free-kick inside his own penalty-area, all of the opposing players shall be at least ten yards (9.15m) from the ball and shall remain outside the penalty-area until the ball has been kicked out of the area. The ball shall be in play immediately it has travelled the distance of its own circumference and is beyond the penalty-area. The goalkeeper shall not receive the ball into his hands, in order that he may thereafter kick it into play. If the ball is not kicked direct into play, beyond the penalty-area, the kick shall be retaken.

When a player is taking a direct or an indirect free-kick outside his own penalty-area, all of the opposing players shall be at least ten yards from the ball, until it is in play, unless they are standing on their own goal-line, between the goal-posts. The ball shall be in play when it has travelled the distance of its own circumference.

If a player of the opposing side encroaches into the penalty-area, or within ten yards of the ball, as the case may be, before a free-kick is taken, the Referee shall delay the taking of the kick, until the Law is complied with.

The ball must be stationary when a free-kick is taken, and the kicker shall not play the ball a second time, until it has been touched or played by another player.

Notwithstanding any other reference in these Laws to the point from which a free-kick is to be taken:

(a) Any free-kick awarded to the defending team, within its own goal area, may be taken from any point within that half of the goal area in which the free-kick has been awarded.

(b) Any indirect free-kick awarded to the attacking team within its opponent's goal area shall be taken from the part of the goal area line which runs parallel to the goal-line, at the point nearest to where the offence was committed.

Punishment. If the kicker, after taking the free-kick, plays the ball a second time before it has been touched or played by another player an indirect free-kick shall be taken by a player of the opposing team from the spot where the infringement occurred, unless the offence is committed by a player in his opponents' goal area, in which case, the free-kick shall be taken from a point anywhere within that half of the goal area in which the offence occurred.

INTERNATIONAL BOARD DECISIONS

1. In order to distinguish between a direct and an indirect free-kick, the Referee, when he awards an indirect free-kick, shall indicate accordingly by raising an arm above his head. He shall keep his arm in that position until the kick has been taken and retain the signal until the ball has been played or touched by another player or goes out of play.

2. Players who do not retire to the proper distance when a free-kick is taken must be cautioned and on any repetition be ordered off. It is particularly requested of Referees that attempts to delay the taking of a free-kick by encroaching should be treated as serious misconduct.

3. If, when a free-kick is being taken, any of the players dance about or gesticulate in a way calculated to distract their opponents, it shall be deemed ungentlemanly conduct for which the offender(s) shall be cautioned.

LAW 14

PENALTY-KICK

A penalty-kick shall be taken from the penalty-mark and, when it is being taken, all players with the exception of the player taking the kick, and the opposing goalkeeper, shall be within the field of play but outside the penalty-area, and at least 10 yards from the penalty-mark. The opposing goalkeeper must stand (without moving his feet) on his own goal-line, between the goal-posts, until the ball is kicked. The player taking the kick must kick the ball forward; he shall not play the ball a second time until it has been touched or played by another player. The ball shall be deemed in play directly it is kicked, i.e., when it has travelled the distance of its circumference. A goal may be scored directly from a penalty-kick. When a penalty-kick is being taken during the normal course of play, or when time has been extended at half-time or full-time to allow a penalty-kick to be taken or retaken, a goal shall not be nullified if, before passing between the posts and under the cross-bar, the ball touches either or both of the goal-posts, or the cross-bar, or the goal-keeper, or any combination of these agencies, providing that no other infringement has occurred.

Punishment:

For any infringement of this Law:

(*a*) by the defending team, the kick shall be retaken if a goal has not resulted;

(*b*) by the attacking team, other than by the player taking the kick, if a goal is scored it shall be disallowed and the kick retaken.

(*c*) by the player taking the penalty-kick, committed after the ball is in play, a player of the opposing team shall take an indirect free-kick from the spot where the infringement occurred, subject to the over-riding conditions imposed in Law 13.

If, in the case of paragraph (c), the offence is committed by the player in his opponents' goal area, the free-kick shall be taken from a point anywhere within that half of the goal area in which the offence occurred.

INTERNATIONAL BOARD DECISIONS

1. When the Referee has awarded a penalty-kick, he shall not signal for it to be taken until the players have taken up position in accordance with the Law.

2. (*a*) If, after the kick has been taken, the ball is stopped in its course towards goal, by an outside agent, the kick shall be retaken.

(*b*) If, after the kick has been taken, the ball rebounds into play, from the goal-keeper, the cross-bar or a goal-post, and is then stopped in its course by an out-side agent, the Referee shall stop play and restart it by dropping the ball at the place where it came into contact with the outside agent, unless it was within the goal area at that time, in which case it shall be dropped on that part of the goal area line which runs parallel to the goal line, at the point nearest to where the ball was when play was stopped.

3. (*a*) If, after having given the signal for a penalty-kick to be taken, the Referee sees that the goalkeeper is not in his right place on the goal-line, he shall, neverthe-less, allow the kick to proceed. It shall be retaken, if a goal is not scored.

(*b*) If, after the Referee has given the signal for the penalty-kick to be taken, and before the ball has been kicked, the goalkeeper moves his feet, the Referee shall, nevertheless, allow the kick to proceed. It shall be retaken, if a goal is not scored.

(*c*) If, after the Referee has given the signal for a penalty-kick to be taken, and before the ball is in play, a player of the defending team encroaches into the penalty-area, or within ten yards of the penalty-mark, the Referee shall, nevertheless, allow the kick to proceed. It shall be retaken, if a goal is not scored.

The player concerned shall be cautioned.

4. (*a*) If, when a penalty-kick is being taken, the player taking the kick is guilty of ungentlemanly conduct, the kick, if already taken, shall be retaken, if a goal is scored.

The player concerned shall be cautioned.

(*b*) If, after the Referee has given the signal for a penalty-kick to be taken, and before the ball is in play, a colleague of the player taking the kick encroaches into the penalty-area or within ten yards of the penalty-mark, the Referee shall, never-theless, allow the kick to proceed. If a goal is scored, it shall be disallowed, and the kick retaken.

The player concerned shall be cautioned.

(*c*) If, in the circumstances described in the foregoing paragraph, the ball rebounds into play from the goalkeeper, the cross-bar or a goal-post, the Referee shall stop the game, caution the player and award an indirect free-kick to the opposing team from the place where the infringement occurred, subject to the over-riding conditions imposed in Law 13.

5. (*a*) If, after the referee has given the signal for a penalty-kick to be taken, and before the ball is in play, the goalkeeper moves from his position on the goal-line, or

moves his feet, and a colleague of the kicker encroaches into the penalty-area or within 10 yards of the penalty-mark, the kick, if taken, shall be retaken.

The colleague of the kicker shall be cautioned.

(b) If, after the Referee has given the signal for a penalty-kick to be taken, and before the ball is in play, a player of each team encroaches into the penalty-area, or within 10 yards of the penalty-mark, the kick, if taken, shall be retaken.

The players concerned shall be cautioned.

6. When a match is extended, at half-time or full-time to allow a penalty-kick to be taken or retaken, the extension shall last until the moment that the penalty-kick has been completed, i.e. until the Referee has decided whether or not a goal is scored, and the game shall terminate immediately the Referee has made his decision.

After the player taking the penalty-kick has put the ball into play, no player other than the defending goalkeeper may play or touch the ball before the kick is completed.

7. When a penalty-kick is being taken in extended time:—

(a) the provisions of all the foregoing paragraphs, except paragraphs 2 (b) and 4 (c) shall apply in the usual way, and

(b) in the circumstances described in paragraphs 2 (b) and 4 (c) the game shall terminate immediately the ball rebounds from the goalkeeper, the cross-bar or the goal-post.

LAW 15

THROW-IN

When the whole of the ball passes over a touch-line, either on the ground or in the air, it shall be thrown in from the point where it crossed the line, in any direction, by a player of the team opposite to that of the player who last touched it. The thrower at the moment of delivering the ball must face the field of play and part of each foot shall be either on the touch-line or on the ground outside the touch-line. The thrower shall use both hands and shall deliver the ball from behind and over his head. The ball shall be in play immediately it enters the field of play, but the thrower shall not again play the ball until it has been touched or played by another player. A goal shall not be scored direct from a throw-in.

Punishment:

(a) If the ball is improperly thrown in the throw-in shall be taken by a player of the opposing team.

(b) If the thrower plays the ball a second time before it has been touched or played by

126

another player, an indirect free-kick shall be taken by a player of the opposing team from the place where the infringement occurred, subject to the over-riding conditions imposed in Law 13.

INTERNATIONAL BOARD DECISIONS

1. If a player taking a throw-in, plays the ball a second time by handling it **within the field of play** before it has been touched or played by another player, the Referee shall award a direct free-kick.

2. A player taking a throw-in must face the field of play with some part of his body.

3. If, when a throw-in is being taken, any of the opposing players dance about or gesticulate in a way calculated to distract or impede the thrower, it shall be deemed ungentlemanly conduct, for which the offender(s) shall be cautioned.

4. A throw-in taken from any position other than the point where the ball passed over the touchline shall be considered to have been improperly thrown in.

LAW 16

GOAL-KICK

When the whole of the ball passes over the goal-line excluding that portion between the goal-posts, either in the air or on the ground, having last been played by one of the attacking team, it shall be kicked direct into play beyond the penalty-area from a point within that half of the goal-area nearest to where it crossed the line, by a player of the defending team. A goalkeeper shall not receive the ball into his hands from a goal-kick in order that he may thereafter kick it into play. If the ball is not kicked beyond the penalty-area, i.e., direct into play, the kick shall be retaken. The kicker shall not play the ball a second time until it has touched or been played by another player. A goal shall not be scored direct from such a kick. Players of the team opposing that of the player taking the goal-kick shall remain outside the penalty-area until the ball has been kicked out of the penalty-area.

Punishment:

If a player taking a goal-kick plays the ball a second time after it has passed beyond the penalty-area, but before it has touched or been played by another player, an indirect free-kick shall be awarded to the opposing team, to be taken from the place where the infringement occurred, subject to the over-riding conditions imposed in Law 13.

INTERNATIONAL BOARD DECISIONS

1. When a goal-kick has been taken and the player who has kicked the ball, touches it again before it has left the penalty-area, the kick has not been taken in accordance with the Law and must be retaken.

LAW 17

CORNER-KICK

When the whole of the ball passes over the goal-line, excluding that portion between the goal-posts, either in the air or on the ground, having last been played by one of the defending team, a member of the attacking team shall take a corner-kick, i.e., the whole of the ball shall be placed within the quarter circle at the nearest corner flag-post, which must not be moved, and it shall be kicked from that position. A goal may be scored direct from such a kick. Players of the team opposing that of the player taking the corner-kick shall not approach within 10 yards of the ball until it is in play, i.e., it has travelled the distance of its own circumference, nor shall the kicker play the ball a second time until it has been touched or played by another player.

Punishment

    (*a*) If the player who takes the kick plays the ball a second time before it has been touched or played by another player, the Referee shall award an indirect free-kick to the opposing team, to be taken from the place where the infringement occurred, subject to the over-riding conditions imposed in Law 13.

    (*b*) For any other infringement the kick shall be retaken.